Dear Parent:
Your child's love of reading starts here!

Every child learns to read in a different way and at his or her own speed. Some go back and forth between reading levels and read favorite books again and again. Others read through each level in order. You can help your young reader improve and become more confident by encouraging his or her own interests and abilities. From books your child reads with you to the first books he or she reads alone, there are I Can Read Books for every stage of reading:

SHARED READING
Basic language, word repetition, and whimsical illustrations, ideal for sharing with your emergent reader

BEGINNING READING
Short sentences, familiar words, and simple concepts for children eager to read on their own

READING WITH HELP
Engaging stories, longer sentences, and language play for developing readers

READING ALONE
Complex plots, challenging vocabulary, and high-interest topics for the independent reader

ADVANCED READING
Short paragraphs, chapters, and exciting themes for the perfect bridge to chapter books

I Can Read Books have introduced children to the joy of reading since 1957. Featuring award-winning authors and illustrators and a fabulous cast of beloved characters, I Can Read Books set the standard for beginning readers.

A lifetime of discovery begins with the magical words **"I Can Read!"**

Visit www.icanread.com for information
on enriching your child's reading experience.

Library of Congress catalog card number: 2006935089
ISBN-13: 978-0-06-088831-2 — ISBN-10: 0-06-088831-8

❖

First Edition

10 11 12 13 14 LP/WOR 20 19 18

TRANSFORMERS™
MEET THE AUTOBOTS

Adapted by Jennifer Frantz
Illustrations by Guido Guidi
Based on the Screenplay by Roberto Orci & Alex
Kurtzman from a Story by Roberto Orci & Alex Kurtzman
and John Rogers

HarperCollinsPublishers

The Autobots are Transformers.

They fight for good and freedom.

Their planet, Cybertron,

was destroyed in a battle

with the evil Decepticons.

Now they have landed on Earth!

The Autobots are searching

for a new home.

They are also looking

for something else. . . .

MISSION

To find the Allspark,
the core of all robot life force,
before the Decepticons do.

Bumblebee gets a cool new shape, too!

Bumblebee is happy

when his friend Sam smiles.

But danger is just around the corner.

This is not a real cop on patrol!

Bumblebee transforms

into a supersonic bad-guy blaster.

With a fast move,

he saves his human pals

from a deadly Decepticon.

A huge truck charges

through the darkness.

But this is no ordinary truck.

It is Optimus Prime—

leader of the Autobots!

He is strong and good.

Optimus Prime calls

his Autobot friends.

Jazz is Optimus Prime's
right-hand man.
He is loyal and brave.

16

No one can top Jazz's speed and style.

17

Ironhide knows all about fighting.

He is one tough Autobot!

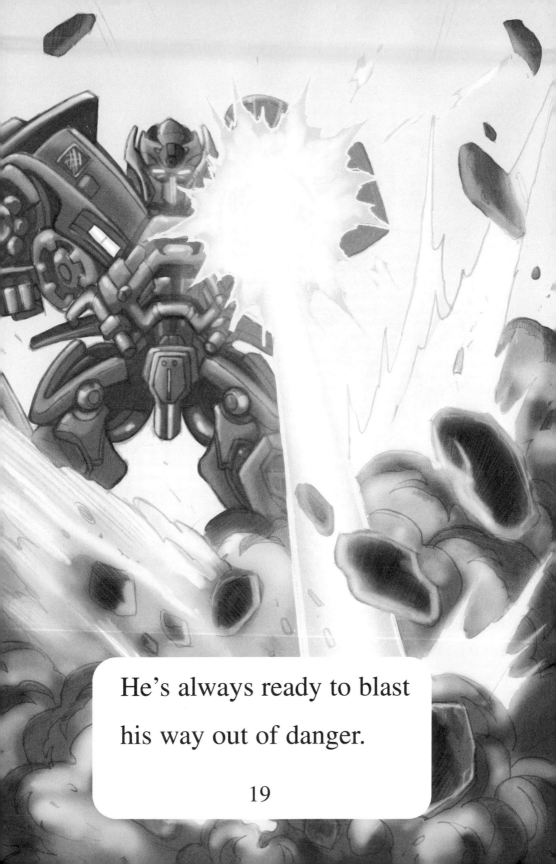

He's always ready to blast
his way out of danger.

19

Ratchet can see trouble

a mile away.

He has X-ray vision!

Ratchet is the rescue truck.

He is always there to help a friend.

"Autobots: Roll out!"

Optimus Prime orders.

It's time to find the Allspark and stop the evil Decepticons.

Yikes! The Autobots are trapped.

But it's nothing a powerful pulse blast

can't handle!

Using a little teamwork,
they get rid of the threat.

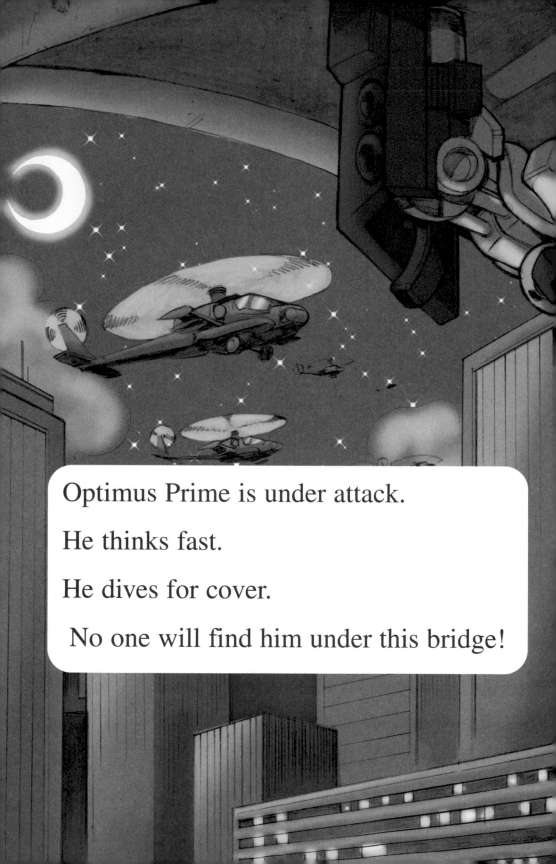

Optimus Prime is under attack.

He thinks fast.

He dives for cover.

No one will find him under this bridge!

The Autobots battle the Decepticons

for the Allspark.

Bumblebee takes a bad hit,

but he will be okay.

Optimus Prime swoops in to save Sam.

And Sam saves the Allspark!

Optimus Prime fights to the end.

Optimus Prime and the Autobots have saved Earth.
In return, the Autobots have a new planet to call home.